The Mysterious Catacombs of World War II

Shaurya Zutshi

Copyright © <2025> <Shaurya Zutshi>

Made with ❤ on the Notion Press Platform

www.notionpress.com

Content

Contents

Foreword

This gripping story takes readers on a thrilling journey through the mysterious catacombs of Paris, seen through the eyes of a young and determined investigator. What begins as a simple curiosity quickly turns into a complex web of secrets, technology, and danger. With vivid imagination and courage, the author builds suspense that keeps you turning pages. This book is a testament to creative storytelling and youthful insight, and I'm proud to present it to you. May it inspire more stories filled with curiosity, courage, and the quest for truth.

Preface

This story began as a spark of curiosity and a deep fascination with mysteries that lie beneath the surface—quite literally. Set against the eerie, historical backdrop of the Paris catacombs, this story follows a young investigator, Robin, whose determination and courage drive him into an underground world filled with secrets, danger, and government conspiracies. As the plot unfolds, what seems like an urban legend turns into a powerful narrative of truth-seeking and resilience.

This book is not just about suspense or action—it's also about friendship, trust, and the impact of daring to ask questions. With a mix of imagination and real-world elements, I've tried to build a world that's thrilling yet relatable. I hope readers—young and old—enjoy the twists, uncover the layers, and feel inspired to believe in the power of investigation, curiosity, and speaking up.

Thank you for choosing to read this story.

Acknowledgments

I would like to express my deepest gratitude to everyone who supported me in bringing *The Mysterious Catacombs of World War II* to life.

First and foremost, I sincerely thank my **parents**, whose love, patience, and constant encouragement gave me the strength and confidence to complete this story. Your unwavering belief in me means the world.

I am also truly grateful to my **teachers**, who helped shape my thoughts, guided my writing, and inspired me to think creatively. Your lessons taught me more than just words—you taught me how to express ideas and bring stories to life.

To those who inspired, listened, and supported me—thank you for being part of this journey. Your motivation helped me dive deep into history, mystery, and imagination.

Writing this book has been an exciting adventure, and I hope it inspires others to explore, question, and create.

This story is a small tribute to all who helped make it possible.

Prologue

Beneath the vibrant streets of Paris lies a forgotten world—one carved from stone, shadow, and secrets. For centuries, the catacombs have whispered tales of the past, but some stories were never meant to be found.

When whispers of strange disappearances reach the ears of young investigator Robin, curiosity quickly turns into obsession. Armed with determination, a digital map, and a thirst for truth, Robin teams up with Sara, an architect with hidden knowledge, and Julius, a tech genius with a mysterious past.

As the trio descends into the tunnels once used during **World War II**, they uncover signs of a deeper conspiracy—one that stretches across continents and decades. What begins as a simple investigation soon becomes a race against time, truth, and powerful forces determined to keep the past buried.

The journey starts now, in the dark heart of Paris, where every step could uncover a secret... or cost them everything.

Chapter 1: The Mystery Begins

I had always dreamt of solving a case that would make me famous in Paris. As a young investigator named ROBIN, clever and curious, I hadn't found a real mystery—until now. Whispers around the city spoke of strange disappearances in the catacombs beneath Paris. People entered… and never came out. I knew this could be the case I'd been waiting for.

One day, when I was still learning about the catacombs, I met Sara in a subway and saw her talking to a person about the catacombs. I became curious and thought that I should talk about the underground tunnels secretly with her because the government had put many restrictions on what people could know and not know about these underground tunnels. Questions were raised to the government which were yet to be answered. But recently, many thrill-seekers and people who wanted answers could not wait for the government. Still, no answers came back; instead, more questions came about these tunnels because none of those people were ever seen again. But now, I wanted answers, and this led me to Sara, who could answer some of my questions.

Chapter 2: The Secret Meeting

Sara told me to come to a little coffee shop right across the street to talk with her. We had a seat in the corner of the coffee shop. She showed me a map of the catacombs. There were many areas pointed out and coloured differently. Colours were used to indicate certain parts of the catacombs. We were searching some ancient and some French catacombs that were used in World War II by the French army and some more tunnels where people went recently.

They had put a tracker and some radar systems, heat detectors, and some more equipment that could be seen by some people, but some of the records were missing or could not be found. But Sara had one record from the early 2000s about four people—out of which two people were inside the tunnels and two were gathering information from outside.

The technology of that period was not great, but she could answer some of the questions. One was that it was not cursed or haunted, but there were noises of guns and people giving orders to capture them. Sara said that she could get this clip from an old member of that team of investigators. He said that he escaped from there with only this one clip, but it could answer two questions—that the tunnels were not haunted nor cursed. Till then, our coffee had arrived. We drank it.

She told me to meet her in her office the next day at 1 a.m. As I was then going home, I went to a bakery for some bread. When I entered the bakery, there was a small television on which some news about the French army traveling to Paris to research the catacombs and the people who went inside these underground tunnels was being shown. I bought a loaf of bread and then went home. But now I think that I may know what is happening in there.

Chapter 3: Forming the Team

I called Sara and planned to go inside these tunnels, but Sara said that we should have someone who can record and detect all the movements that we make inside these tunnels. I asked her who could help us to do such work from above. Sara said she just might know a person who could help us.

She waited for some minutes and then said a name—**JULIUS!!!!!!** She said he is a tech genius who can help us with giving us information and needed advice. Robin said, "So you should talk with him." Sara said, "Okay, I will talk to him."

Several days had passed. Sara was not responding. Till then, I was watching each step of the French army. But one day, she responded and said all the equipment was ready and Julius had agreed to help us.

"Meet me in front of the Eiffel Tower tomorrow at 9 a.m., and I will introduce you to Julius." I reached in front of the Eiffel Tower and met Julius and Sara.

Sara said, "This is Julius, our tech expert, who will guide us inside the tunnels and give us suggestions." I asked if he lived in Paris. Sara replied that he was from Lyon. We both decided that he should have a code name, and his code name was decided to be **PLAYER**.

All three of us moved to the office to discuss our plan.

Chapter 4: The Hidden Bunker

We reached her office. I didn't know that Sara was an architect, but she revealed an underground room—not a normal room—a big area that could do all the functions of a normal house.

Sara said, "I have also made some tunnels that can connect us with some of the catacombs. It can help us go inside them anytime we want."

I asked, "Do you go inside them frequently?"

Sara said, "No, I cannot go there frequently because there is danger. Who knows what's lurking in those mysterious dark tunnels? When I was digging, I also found a very old 19th-century sewer."

I investigated and found that the sewer was connected to the catacombs. We could safely travel anywhere we wanted without entering from the surface.

PLAYER said, "I can locate the certain areas where the strangest phenomena have been recorded and put some devices that can detect heat signals and can record all the audio."

Sara and I said, "Good idea." I also said, "Can I also go with Julius? I can see the catacombs and talk with him as we've just met today."

Sara said, "Fine, we will do this tomorrow."

Chapter 5: The News Leak

Meanwhile, I switched on the television and was shocked to see that all the news channels were showing Sara and me in the coffee shop where we had first discussed the catacombs. I quickly called Julius and Sara.

They came and saw that somebody in the café had made a video of us talking about the catacombs. Sara and I knew that the French intelligence agency D.G.S.E would be tracking our every move now.

Sara said, "We cannot go to a public place or else the French intelligence will catch us."

I said, "Everyone should take their prized belongings from their house and bring them to this bunker before dawn."

Sara and I immediately went to our homes under the cover of darkness. Meanwhile, Julius was in the bunker. He didn't have to leave because now he was the only one in the team no one knew about.

Sara and I brought everything most valuable to us and that we could carry. We arrived at the bunker minutes before dawn.

I brought a suitcase, some video games, and my pet **OREO**, my dog. Sara also brought her suitcase and important documents. She was surprised to know that I had a dog. She had loved dogs since she was little.

Till then, Julius was investigating the tunnels. He said that there was also a possibility that the same place was where young wizards attended school.

Sara said, "No, it's unlikely."

I said, "Yes, it can be. Maybe it's like a real Harry Potter school down there."

Sara and I started unpacking our belongings.

Chapter 6: Strange Discoveries

Everyone started to prepare for what was to come. Suddenly, a break in the story came.

Julius had attached some cameras in the 19th-century sewer that Sara found while digging. Some cameras caught French intelligence. There were some trucks in which handcuffed people were being transported.

When he researched it, he found out that they were from the family of the Italian mafia. Sara was confused—why were criminals being transported through these tunnels and where were they being taken?

I said, "We need answers fast. Tomorrow early morning, we'll see what's in those tunnels."

Julius said, "Yes, I have put many cameras and everything we'll need in the catacombs."

Sara also agreed and said, "Yes, we must do something. The government knows about us."

Chapter 7: Into the Catacombs

So, the next day, everything was ready. All the equipment was packed. Sara and I geared up, and Julius started recording, rebooted, and switched on his devices.

Sara, Julius, and I said to each other, "Good luck," and then Sara and I went inside the catacombs. We had a digital map from which we could get a visual of the mapped parts of the catacombs.

We headed to the place where the French intelligence was found transporting criminals. The mapped section of the catacombs was about to end, and we were entering new turf.

We checked if all the devices were on and tested our microphones, then asked if Julius could see and record on all the cameras. Julius said, "Yes," and then we proceeded to move into the unmapped part of the catacombs.

For some hours, absolutely no sound came. It was a little too silent. The local time was 8:00 a.m. Suddenly, we heard the sound of trucks.

Sara and I finished our croissants and drank our tea. We were hiding behind large rocks that had fallen from the ceiling of the sewer. The truck was about to pass where we were.

We quickly threw a rope with a machine. It grabbed a piece of the truck and dragged us to it.

Chapter 8: The Cargo Ship

Julius analyzed and saw that the truck model had a metal door. He didn't know whether it was locked or not. It was a gamble.

We didn't have any more well-planned ideas. Luckily, the door was open and there was no one in the back side of the truck.

Julius also saw the timing of the truck when there were people inside and analyzed where and when it was going.

Sara and I checked the time and knew this was the time when the criminals were being transported. We waited for four hours in the truck.

Many checkpoints came, but no one suspected there was anyone in the back. We had arrived. It was a port in Lyon.

Luckily, all cameras and audio were working perfectly from so far. We exited the truck the same way we had entered, hiding at the bottom.

A huge cargo ship was parked there. We guessed the ship was going to the place where the other criminals were transported. We had to make a choice.

So, when no one was looking, we made our move to the cargo ship. It was about to leave.

We found an empty cargo container and got inside. The ship was beginning to move.

Chapter 9: The Long Journey

We talked to Julius. He said, "Can you show me any numbers or details written on the ship?"

Luckily, there was a window in our container. We showed him the pattern and designs on the ship.

He took some time but found the owner and destination. The ship had many stops: Spain, Mexico, and the final stop was the United States of America. And the owner of the ship was the government of France.

The sun was going to set. Sara and I made a bed from hay and tried to make a pillow by placing our bags on top.

It wasn't the coziest, but it did the job. We made a schedule—one of us would sleep for an hour while the other kept watch.

We continued this for six days. One night, Sara heard someone walking near the container.

But luckily, it was just someone going to the washroom.

The ship ported in Spain and Mexico. Some new people boarded—more bad guys.

Now we understood why this container was empty. It wasn't transporting goods—it was transporting criminals to the U.S.A.

But why? We still didn't know.

After some days, many people started to die, and two days later, we were the only ones still alive on the cargo ship.

We contacted Julius and told him everything.

He told us to abandon the vessel immediately.

Sara and I took an emergency boat. Mysteriously, it had just enough fuel to reach the U.S.A.

We noted the numbers and patterns on it, threw all the fuel into the sea, and left.

But Sara wasn't buying it. She knew something was odd.

Chapter 10: The Truth Revealed

We reached a countryside and found more empty vessels and an old port. It looked like no one was there.

Sara spotted the management office. We entered and went to the records section.

Sara remembered that sometime ago, she read about a protocol in which, when the U.S.A and French governments realized there had been a breach, they would initiate certain actions—just like what was happening now.

Sara quickly realized and said, "This is the protocol I read about."

I said, "So we have to do something quickly."

We were looking for anything that might help us crack the case when suddenly I saw something—a file about the French catacombs.

I said to Sara, "I found something about the catacombs."

She said, "We should quickly escape from here. The army would be on their way."

Suddenly, Julius came with a boat and said, "Hop on." We sped toward a small airport on a nearby island.

I asked him, "What are you doing here?"

Julius said, "It's a long story, but now we have to head to the plane."

We reached the island and boarded the plane.

Julius said, "We will reach Paris in one hour."

Sara and I asked him what was going on.

Julius said, "You have solved the mystery."

I said, "So I won't be needing this book any time soon."

Julius explained that protests had started against the French government.

"While you guys were investigating, I realized why the people were disappearing for so long. They had been disappearing because the French government was using the catacombs to smuggle criminals to the U.S.A and then wipe them off the record. You two just exposed everything."

<u>About the Author</u>

Shaurya Zutshi is a young and passionate writer with a keen eye for looking at the world through a unique lens. He believes in exploring topics that are often overlooked or rarely discussed, giving voice to stories that deserve attention. Shaurya has a deep love for history and enjoys diving into the lesser-known events, people, and mysteries that have shaped our past. This book is a reflection of his curiosity and dedication to understanding history beyond textbooks. When he's not reading or writing, Shaurya spends his time researching unusual historical facts and sharing them with others. Through his writing, he hopes to inspire young readers to think differently, question deeply, and always stay curious.